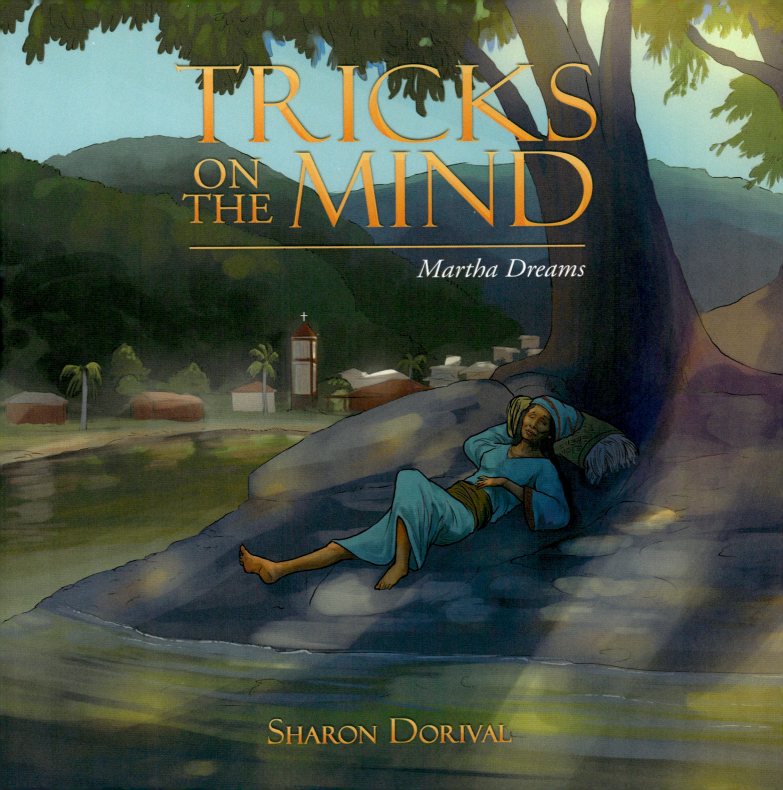

Print information available on the last page

Rev. date: 02/06/2019

To order additional copies of this book, contact:
Xlibris
1-888-795-4274
www.Xlibris.com
Orders@Xlibris.com

TRICKS ON THE MIND

By Sharon Dorival

There's a thin line between dreams and reality.
-Sharon Dorival, Camrose 2015

INTRODUCTION

Since 1985, it has been my privilege to meet with and listen to storytellers from around the world. Most times our encounters were simply to sit and talk about stories that have affected our lives. Sometimes it was just to encourage each other to participate in oral storytelling.Other times it was to encourage others to pick up the pen or record a snippet of a song or recite a poem. As a result these people have shared wonderful stories with me- Stories about roosters and children, airplanes and typewriters. Stories about fireworks and festivals, happiness and challenges.

Many of my collected work are based on the stories that the villagers of Colihaut have shared with me during our time together. Most of them are accounts of things that have occurred, but others are fictions rooted in personal experiences and still others are stories told as poems. All of the stories are filled with the wisdom and love shared over the course of many years.

May you learn as much as I have from these threads of love and may they bring you as much joy as well.

Happy Reading!!!!!!
Sharon Dorival
Camrose, Alberta, 2017

Martha is a tall slender dark skinned girl with natural long, curly hair. She resembles her grandmother and always has her head wrapped in beautiful coloured cloths and wore beautiful dresses to match her head ties.

Martha's dad is a Carib Indian hence her long curly hair.
Martha's mom is an African woman hence Martha's choice of clothing.
Martha's grandfather was a mulatto and a devout Catholic.
Martha's aunty was a white woman and a Protestant.
The Health Care Aide was a Syrian.

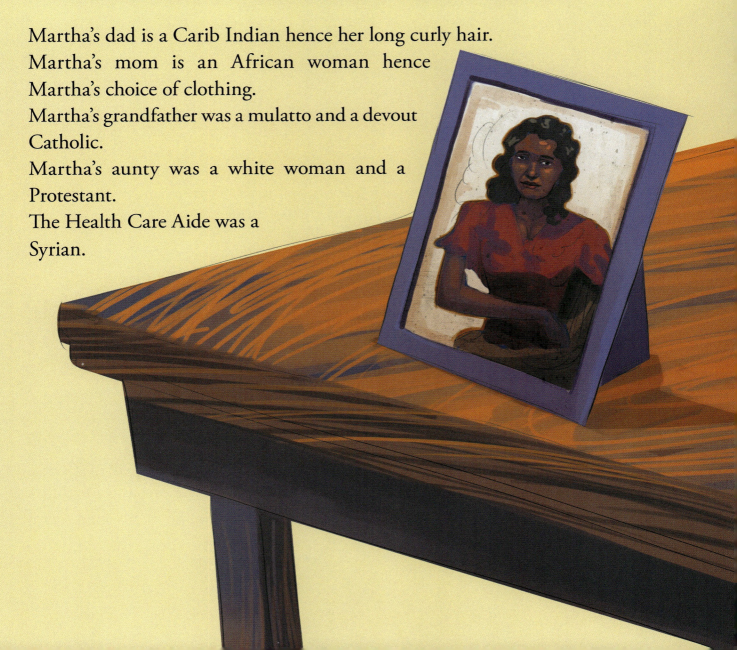

In the dream,
Martha saw her dad. He had gone to be with his maker The Lord and Savior for 2 years now since August 2014. While he was laying at home he mentioned seeing his sister, who had passed on a few years before him, in the room that Martha's mom had put him in to rest.

In the dream, he was explaining to Martha that he saw his sister come in and started cleaning his room.

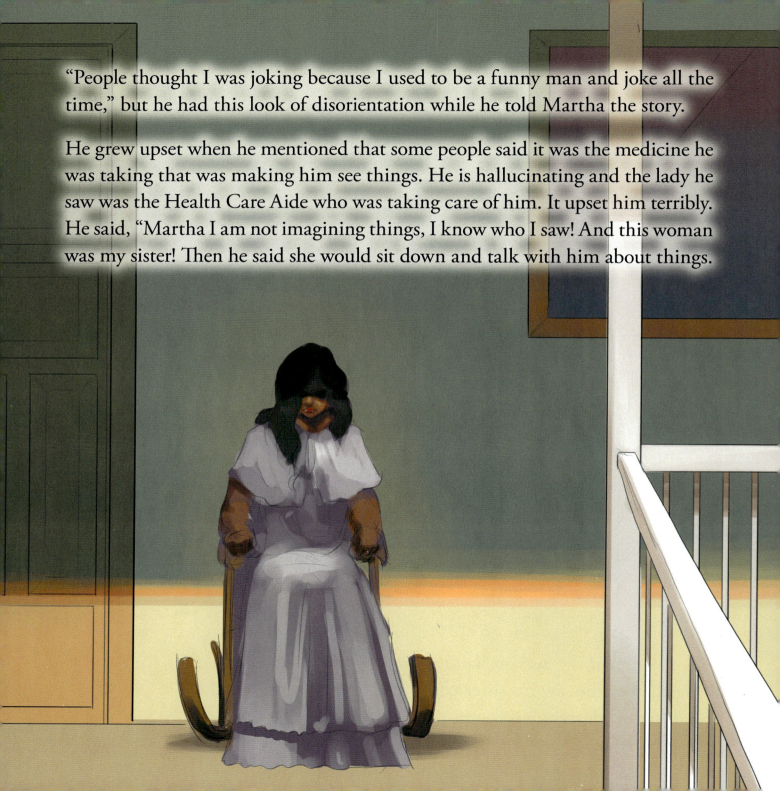

"People thought I was joking because I used to be a funny man and joke all the time," but he had this look of disorientation while he told Martha the story.

He grew upset when he mentioned that some people said it was the medicine he was taking that was making him see things. He is hallucinating and the lady he saw was the Health Care Aide who was taking care of him. It upset him terribly. He said, "Martha I am not imagining things, I know who I saw! And this woman was my sister! Then he said she would sit down and talk with him about things.

Serious things Martha. Life. What's important."

Martha woke up thinking that she felt a presence in her room that was not there before, Was she imagining things? Was her aunty here to comfort her as she did for her dad? This is weird, thought Martha. No one is there. It's just my mind playing tricks on me. She glanced over to where her dad was sitting and waited until he was finished smoking his pipe then she asked him " Dad, what do you feel when your dead sister visits you? This question put a twist on things. He started telling Martha that his Health Care Aide was with him one day when he asked her a question. When she came over he started telling Merlyn about it - She was reading a book while watching him and she said "you have this look again Floyd. You have it all over your face" then she asked me "what was wrong?", he said.

I asked Merlyn, "Can you see it?" and she asked me

"can I see what?" Then I pointed up towards the ceiling and the corner of the walls where all three met and said "that beautiful light!"

She said, "I do not see anything, but describe it to me." So he started telling her it was such a beautiful bright white light, so beautiful he had never seen anything like it before and she asked him

"what was it?"

He said to her, "it is heaven! and this part just made no sense to Martha because she didn't understand how he can be on earth and seeing heaven? But she asked him "how do I get there?" and he said that

"you will be there soon enough." That's all Martha could remember about that dream. He further went on telling her about his experience at the Old Age Home "while I was being treated, the medicine started not to work because of the other medications I was taking, so they had to transfer me to the Hospice, which hurt me because I wanted to be at home when I passed.

I understood, it was so they could give me stronger medicine to control my pain, while there, My sister kept visiting me.She would come and see me and prayed silently over me then we would talk softly to each other and then she would just lay her hands over mine and hold my hands. Then one day, she brought me this beautifully illustrated bible.

While she walked in the healing garden

I sat near the fireplace in my room and started reading Psalm 23, trying to understand what David meant. I read it over and over until a calmness I had never experienced before came over me and comforted me. David told me in his words that I will be ok, that there is no need to continue hurting, that Jesus is there and will take all my pain away. After that my breathing changed and went more up into my chest and my sister stood up behind me with silvery angel wings. And then I slowly took my last breath and went home to be with Jesus. Martha was upset and crying, but she felt so much at peace now that she knew her dad was with Christ without pain and no longer suffering. Later on, she was thinking about Psalms 23 - that was written by King David to help show humans that God is always with us and never leaves our side. Her dad said "Please do not think that I am telling you this story to make it about me in any way, because it's not and never will be. It is about how God's Word can soothe and relax a person who is scared of letting go because he loves his family- his entire family! That he was having such a hard time letting go and was willing to suffer for all his family. And with him reading that we would be okay and the comforting words of God, was all he needed to put him at ease. Martha loved Psalm 23 and when she broke it down to attain the meaning of her dream, it clearly states "never be afraid for I Am Christ Jesus here with you and I will never let you go. I Am Always Here With You! And you will dwell in the House of the Lord

Forever!!!"

This story takes place in the beautiful village of Colihaut. Colihaut is a village on the West Coast of the Commonwealth of Dominica.

Dominica must not be mistaken for the Dominican Republic.

Let Us Learn About Colihaut
- Colihaut is a village in the Commonwealth of Dominica and sits comfortably in the parish of Saint Peter.

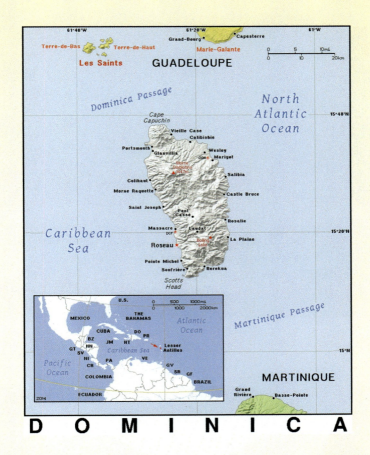

D O M I N I C A

- Colihaut is also a coastal village in Northern Dominica and has a population of 773 people.
- Colihaut beach is primarily gray sand with smooth waters flaked by mountain ranges. It is a great place to enjoy the sunset or watch fishermen heading home with their catch over the light blue Caribbean Sea.
- Colihaut is home to a primary school, sports field, day nursery, post office, credit union, village council, four churches.
- Residents of Colihaut earn a living mainly through agriculture

and fishing.

- Along the banks of the river is a variety of fruit trees: Mangoes with different names

Coconut Trees

Pawpaw

Guavas

Soursop

- Residents of Colihaut can actually survive on the banks of the rivers while completing their chores for the day.
- Colihaut River is very busy with women washing laundry, children playing in the water, or catching crayfish and millets.

REVIEWS FOR TRICKS ON THE MIND

This is the outline of a story that acts as a series of internal dialogues, philosophical discussions, accounts of a traditional lifestyle and, above all, elaborate descriptions of a village on a tropical Island. The dream allowed Floyd and Martha to be what they could not be. Martha is confronting her fears and by doing so she learned to accept the emotions she had been repressing. I think her dreams were somewhat therapeutic and she used them to help others in her community. Some might argue that Floyd being a Carib Indian was just drunk and was indeed hallucinating. Martha probably took her father's traits and this dream could mean nothing more than just the vivid imagination of a teenage girl. Was it just fantastical living? Martha wanted more than she had and could have offered her father. She longed to find ways to ease his miseries while he was alive and now he has returned to give her a second chance but she is only dreaming, lol. There are so many other things though. The green trees in the dream could symbolize Protection, strength and growth in Martha's life. She could be getting wiser. Thinking of the family tree, the trees could mean that she has strong family ties. It all depends on the way the branches stand, we could have a totally different meaning. Let's look at the river. Rivers create moods: Water is life. So it could mean life is passing Martha by but it seems like this river brought prosperity to this village. What would life in Colihaut be without it? This river was busy though not chaotic so it could mean that Martha's life was calm, busy and full. Who knows? Also seeing that she dreamt about an elderly could be a sign of luck, virtue and maybe thoughts of a long life. Breaking this dream down could make a different story of its own. Let's look at the environment especially the healing garden. The author didn't say what kind of plants were in there but plants have always been used for medication purposes. Some for beauty, some for love, some to healing different parts of the body. The best, best thing to do is to visit this village and explore the various ways to heal. Though this is a dream it also has a lot of reality. Cheers to life everyone. Viva Dominica! Respect Colihaut!

~ Patrick Monty

There is a sense of relief as Martha realizes that her father had a normal reaction and he actually wasn't losing his mind. Sure it might have created a lot of anxiety for the people involved namely Merlyn Martha and Floyd but we see real-life situation relating to the death of a loved one. Reference was made to a hospice, a healing garden which I think every dying person should have access to. It takes me right back to Gethsemane where Jesus was before his death. Death and gardens are interrelated. Why wait till the person is dead to create a beautiful garden of flowers and trees for them? That's a really deep dream. Hmm. We see the power of medicine in those needing healing. This is a dream of life itself as is. It's humbling and inspirational. Yes, we see some work but the main thing portrayed was life in the form of trees, the river, people working together, a beautiful community that's calling to everyone. Come to take a break, relax and let go of the stresses of life. Allow yourself to dream. And although it's tiled Tricks on The Mind, it's really not a trick. It is a reality to the core cause life itself is a trick!

~ Nakinda

"This story has inspired me to start writing my own stories. The principle woven into this incredible story has definitely changed my life."

~ Hayleecia Dorival
Student at Ecole Camrose Composite High School

"You will not be the same person after reading this book, Sharon Dorival and her powerfully, inspiring tales have literally changed my life! Her poems, songs and short stories helps me remember what it was like. They are like Soul food. Raw and written from the heart"

~ Hezzy
Student at Ecole Charlie Killam School

"Tricks On The Mind is a story of life, loss and hope. It reminds us of the universal healing experience of letting go."

- Peggy Laurent
Reading Buddy

Printed in the United States
By Bookmasters